Steve was raised by wolves.

Then one day Steve's mom walked him through the woods...

"Steve," his mom said, "I know you're anxious about going to school. It's not always easy to get along with humans, but just be yourself. I know you'll have a great day!"

Steve thought about what his mom had said.

He howled and growled during attendance.

HOOOOOOOOOOOOWL!

He shredded banners and tore down posters in the hallway.

He pounced on other kids.

He gave everyone fleas.

And then there was lunch.

That afternoon,
Steve brought home
a note from his teacher.

Mrs. Wolf,

Steve had a hard time staying out of trouble today.

Mrs. Meadows

"I love that you're being yourself," Steve's mom said. "Can you find a way to get along with everyone else, too?"

But the next day...

...he ate another kid's homework.

He marked his territory on the playground.

He buried Mrs. Meadows's laptop.

He drank from the toilet.

After school, Steve's teacher stopped by the den to speak with his mom.

"Steve," his mom said, "school isn't going away. I know you can make this work. Now, let's go take a flea bath."

Steve thought hard about it.

When Steve got to class the next morning, everyone was in a panic!

He followed his nose under
Mrs. Meadows's desk...

down the hall...

and into the cafeteria,

where he opened
the fridge.

There was Reggie! (He looked delicious.)

The class cheered. The wolf had saved the day.

And Steve finally understood what his mom had been telling him.

For the rest of the day, Steve found new ways to become part of the pack at school—

at recess...

during music...

while the class worked in the garden...

and even at lunch.

When Steve got off the bus,
he had a surprise for his mom.

And she was so proud.

Mrs. Wolf,

Steve had a <u>great</u> day today!

Mrs. Meadows

For my kids, who are part wolf (mother's side)
—J.C.

About This Book

Do you know how hard it is to draw a book while inside a wolf den? I do. The illustrations
for this book were done by hand with ink on paper, but then wolves chewed up the paper.
Once I'd pried the drawings away, I dried, scanned, and colored them digitally,
but only after the wolves got done checking their e-mail.

This book was edited by Andrea Spooner and Deirdre Jones and designed by Phil Caminiti
with art direction by Patti Ann Harris. The production was supervised by Erika Schwartz,
and the production editor was Christine Ma. This book was printed on 128-gsm Gold Sun matte
paper. The text was set in HandySans, and the display type was hand-lettered.